TRUE TALL
TALES OF STORMALONG:
Sailor of the Seven Seas

By Harold W. Felton

Illustrated by Joan Sandin

Prentice-Hall, Inc., Englewood Cliffs, N. J.

Other Books by Harold W. Felton

BOWLEG BILL: *SEAGOING COWPUNCHER*
PECOS BILL AND THE MUSTANG
NEW TALL TALES OF PECOS BILL

LEGENDS OF PAUL BUNYAN.
JOHN HENRY AND HIS HAMMER
FIRE-FIGHTIN' MOSE
COWBOY JAMBOREE
EDWARD ROSE, NEGRO TRAILBLAZER
JAMES P. BECKWOURTH, NEGRO MOUNTAIN MAN
MIKE FINK—KEELBOATMAN
SERGEANT O'KEEFE AND HIS MULE, BALAAM
THE WORLD'S MOST TRUTHFUL MAN
A HORSE NAMED JUSTIN MORGAN
WILLIAM PHIPS AND THE TREASURE SHIP

Third printing.........September, 1971

TRUE TALL TALES OF STORMALONG: Sailor of the Seven Seas by Harold W. Felton
© 1968 by Harold W. Felton
© 1968 by Prentice-Hall, Inc., for illustrations in this edition
Library of Congress Catalog Card Number: 68-22880
Printed in the United States of America • J
Prentice-Hall International, Inc., London
Prentice-Hall of Australia, Pty. Ltd., Sydney
Prentice-Hall of Canada, Ltd., Toronto
Prentice-Hall of India Private Ltd., New Delhi
Prentice-Hall of Japan, Inc., Tokyo

CONTENTS

For Elisabeth and Gerhard

1.

Little Stormy

His name was Stormalong. He was the greatest sailor ever to sail the seas. He was not like other men, so naturally the details of his birth were not exactly the same as those of other men.

He was born in the middle of a hurricane. Tall hemlocks and pine trees bent low before the wind. Oaks and maples swayed to the gale's wild tune as the storm howled through the trees. Rain washed the world. Thunder roared and waves crashed against the rocks that divided the sea from the land.

All of this tumult made some people think that Stormalong wasn't born at all, that he was created out of thunder and waves, rain, wind, and rocks. But it isn't true. He was born, just like everyone else. Well, almost like everyone else.

Since none of the storks would go out in the terrible storm, one hundred stormy petrels carried the baby toward his birth-place. They carried him in a top mainsail.

But the baby was too heavy for them, and the wing-weary birds were finally forced to make a landing two leagues from their goal.

Something had to be done, and quickly, for a birth was about to take place. So the baby carefully piled the exhausted birds in the middle of the mainsail, gathered the corners to-gether, threw it over his shoulder, and set off for his place of birth.

When he stepped in the door of his birthplace, he put his package of petrels on the warm hearthstone where they could dry out, rest their weary muscles, and fluff their feathers. It was a part of his character to be kind.

Then he turned toward his parents, who were waiting for him, and grinned. The storm lashed at the New England coast with greater fury.

When his mother saw him, she smiled and said, "His eyes are blue and green, blue-green, like the sea."

His father seemed to grow two inches with pride as he gazed into the eyes of his son. "You come from a long line of men who went down to the sea in ships," he said. "They were iron men who sailed wooden ships. You will be a man of iron too."

The neighbors said, "My, what a big baby!"

His parents named him Alfred Bulltop. Alfred Bulltop Stormalong.

7

His mother was right. His father was right. The neighbors were right. Everything they had said about him was true.

He was a big baby, and the neighbors were bug-eyed with amazement when they saw that the baby had a full set of teeth. He was such a big baby his parents had to blow a foghorn to wake him up.

No cradle was big enough for little Stormy, so they used a whaleboat. No room in the house was big enough for a whaleboat, so his father anchored it out in the bay, and that is where he spent the first days of his youth.

There it was that he laughed and played with the sharks when they came close enough for him to reach out and fondle their fins. For a time sharks were his only playmates, and he swam and wrestled with them. He was always careful not to hurt them.

Stormy was a curly-headed lad, with an unruly cowlick and a freckled face. He was a happy baby and seldom caused any trouble. But one day when he was restless he turned over suddenly in his cradle, starting a tidal wave that washed away six lobster shacks and almost wrecked the town pier.

After that he was always careful not to make any sudden movements, although it was very difficult for such a big baby to stay still all the time.

They fed him whale milk and clam chowder and there was plenty of johnnycake, maple syrup, fish, lobster, salt pork, baked beans and brown bread. His appetite was good, and

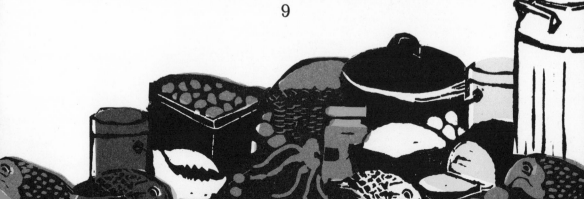

he tucked away great quantities of food. He liked clam chowder especially and ate a lot of it. He spooned it out of a wash tub with a spoon as big as a half-bushel scoop. He grew rapidly, as might be expected.

He was a big help to his father and mother. He knew where the best clam beds were and gathered and shucked clams for the whole family. He ran a string of lobster pots and built up a profitable business selling clams and lobster to the people who lived in the village.

Stormy had salt water in his blood. One day a tall, slender pine tree floated near his cradle. It had been uprooted by a gale. Stormy pulled it out of the water and stripped the branches off. He held it out at arm's length and yelled at it. He yelled so loud the bark peeled off.

Using the tree trunk for a mast and his blanket for a sail, he rigged up his whaleboat cradle as a sailboat. As soon as he got her under way, he turned her prow and put out from the bay, into the ocean.

"Avast and ahoy!" he shouted with glee.

With a voice that sounded like a foghorn he broke into song, as his boat dipped into the troughs and rose to the crests of the waves:

"Oh, a sailor's life is the life for me!"

His mother worried for a while, but she soon came to realize it was less dangerous when he was at play far away from the bay. She remembered the tidal wave he started when he turned over suddenly in his cradle.

Stormy spent the days of his youth, when he was not in school, in his homemade boat, coasting between Nova Scotia and the Gulf of Mexico. He was an excellent student in geography and knew every bay and point, bar, gulf and island on the East Coast.

2.
Stormy Lifts Anchor

Stormy soon outgrew his baby cradle-boat, and as he grew bigger he built and traded for larger and still larger boats. He was out sailing every minute he was not in school or doing his chores.

One morning he took his friend Jonathan out in his boat before school to set some lobster traps. By the time they were through, the rising wind had changed, and the boys faced a long journey home, tacking against the wind for the first leg of their trip. A peninsula two miles long and half a mile wide lay between them and the schoolhouse.

"What are we going to do?" asked Jonathan. "It will take us an hour or more to tack down to the tip of the peninsula before we can come around and sail with the wind at the stern." He gazed sadly over the stretch of land that separated them from the schoolhouse.

"I know what to do," said Stormy. He turned the rudder and the boat came around. The sail filled and bent low as the craft moved directly toward the shore of the peninsula.

"Hey! What are you doing?" Jonathan shouted. "You'll run her aground!"

"Maybe not," said Stormy. "The peninsula is smooth, and it's wet with dew."

"Dew? What has dew got to do with it?"

13

Stormy grinned. Then his lips firmed. He held the rudder steady and kept an eye on the sail. There could be no slack in it. He must keep it full and tight.

The wind stayed with him, and under his expert hand the small craft skimmed over the wet sand of the beach and onto the dew-damp grass. As lightly as a butterfly flitting from flower to flower, the boat sped across the half-mile of peninsula and down into the water on the other side, just in time for school.

The schoolmaster and the other children, who were standing in the schoolyard, were amazed.

"That boy is a real sailor," the schoolmaster said. "A real sailor! He can sail in shallower water than anyone I ever saw or heard of!"

There were other surprises in store for the schoolmaster. No one who saw it ever forgot the time Stormy's father wanted to move an anchor from the warehouse on the north side of town to the shipyard on the south side of town.

Three men couldn't lift it, and the dray wagon was busy hauling lumber. Stormy said, "I'll carry the anchor." He picked it up and marched down the street.

As Stormy passed the inn he met the schoolmaster. "Alfred Bulltop!" the man said. He usually called the boy Alfred, but the sight of Stormy carrying the anchor all alone had unnerved him so much that he added the middle name for emphasis.

"Wha– wha– what are you doing?" The words came out with great difficulty.

Stormy stopped. "Nothing, sir. Just going to the other side of town."

"But what in heaven's name do you have under your arm?" The tone of the schoolmaster's voice made this sound like an accusation, which he did not really intend, because carrying an anchor is an innocent thing.

Stormy looked down. "Oh, that, sir. I had forgotten about that. It's an anchor," he added helpfully. "I'm taking it to the shipyard south of town for my father."

The anchor was so heavy that young Stormalong had sunk up to his ankles in the hard-packed stone road during the discussion.

"Well, I should be going. My father will want the anchor," Stormy said as he lifted his feet out of the holes and walked off down the street.

The schoolmaster gazed at the holes so hard that his eyes stuck out of his head like hard-boiled eggs.

When Stormy was eleven years old he had to start shaving. His beard was as tough as the bristles on a swabbing brush and his hair was as thick and strong as rope yarn. At twelve he finished school.

He studied so hard the last year he was in school that he finished the last three grades in one year. He had to do it because he had grown so much that the seats in the schoolhouse wouldn't have held him if he had stayed another year.

"I'm ready to go," he said.

"Go where?" his father asked.

"Into the world, to find my place in it," Stormy said.

His father and his mother nodded. So did the neighbors and the schoolmaster.

"But where in the world will you go?" his father asked.

"I will go down to the sea in ships. Salt water is in my blood," he said.

"Just like the Stormalongs have always done," his father said. "The ships are wooden ships, but you will be a man of iron."

3.

Stormy Sets Sail

Stormy didn't have far to go. Ships from the seven seas dropped anchor at New England's ports. He gazed over the harbor. A forest of towering masts reached for the sky.

"I want to sail on a big ship," he said to himself. He scanned the thicket of spars that rose from the groups of ships clustered along the wharfs and the vessels anchored here and there in the bay.

His eye caught the tallest masts and he made for them. They were on a four-masted schooner, *Lady of the Sea*.

As he walked up the gang plank, the boards groaned under his weight and the ship leaned toward the dock. Captain Hardstone, sitting in his cabin at work on the ship's manifest, felt the vessel move and rushed topside. "Avast," he cried. "What's wrong with my ship? What has made her lose her trim?"

18

He stood on the slanting deck. Slowly he raised his eyes up Stormy's giant frame. He could hardly believe what he saw. He had never seen anyone so big before. But he was master of his ship and a fearless man. "What do you want?" he roared.

"I want a job," said Stormy.

"I see how big you are, but how old are you?"

"Twelve, going on thirteen."

"That's the right age for a cabin boy, and I need a cabin boy."

"I'm willing to start at the bottom," said Stormy.

"But you're too big for a cabin boy."

"I can do a man's work."

"Don't doubt it a bit," said the captain, "not with your size and all them muscles. What's your name?"

"Alfred Bulltop Stormalong," the boy said as he drew himself up and threw out his chest, breaking some of the seams on his shirt with his bulging muscles.

Captain Hardstone squinted at him. A question was in his eye. "Didn't I see you once in a single-masted small craft off the Silver Shoals to the Nor'ard of Hispaniola?"

"Could be," said Stormy. "I've been there."

"Then again, I think I saw you sailing in the high seas off of Cape Hatteras in a blow."

"No doubt," said Stormy. "I've sailed those seas."

"You have the size of a sailor. More than enough size. And you have the muscle too. More than enough. I have seen you in deep water where few men would dare to sail in a craft so small."

19

The captain paused and ran his thick fingers across his grizzled chin. He closed one eye and studied Stormy through the narrowed slit of the other. "But," he said, "you must be examined."

"Examined?" said Stormy.

"Exactly. Otherwise how would I know if you are suited to be a sailor?"

"I'll take any examination that is necessary."

"Good. Now listen well, for I don't want to repeat any question any more than I want to repeat commands on board my ship," said Captain Hardstone.

"Set your sails and cast off," Stormy said.

"Now then. A terrible storm is coming up on the starboard side. What would you do?" The captain didn't have to wait long for an answer.

"I'd drop the anchor, sir," said Stormy.

The captain didn't pause. "Another gale bears down on you from the stern. What would you do?"

"I'd drop an anchor, sir," said Stormy.

"There is another giant blow coming at you from the port side. What would you do?"

"I'd drop an anchor, sir," said Stormy.

"Still another gale is swirling down on you off the prow. What would you do?"

"Drop an anchor, sir," Stormy said firmly.

"Ah ha!" Captain Hardstone cried as he pounded a fist into his open hand, then lifted it in the form of an accusing finger which he aimed at the young man standing before him.

It was a dramatic moment, and Stormy waited for the next question. "Tell me this!" Captain Hardstone cried. "Where would you get all them anchors? Tell me! Where would you get all them anchors?"

22

There. He had the boy. What would the young man say now?

Young Stormalong didn't pause or bat an eye. "Why, I'd get them in the same place you got all those storms, sir," he said.

Captain Hardstone's accusing finger slowly lost its form and wilted. Then the captain roared with laughter. "Good answer! Fine answer!" he declared. "You'll be a first class sailor. First class! Yes sir!"

He put the stub of a pencil to his log. "I'll sign you on," he said. He started to spell out the words, Alfred Bulltop Stormalong. "No. Your name is too long for my log. Let me see. I know. I'll just put your name down, A.B. Stormalong."

Captain Hardstone bore down heavily as his pencil made the final dot. "There," he said triumphantly. "That makes it A.B.S. That stands for Able Bodied Seaman, as well as Alfred Bulltop Stormalong."

Ever since that time all good sailors have had those initials after their names. A.B.S., for Able Bodied Seaman.

Captain Hardstone could tell that Stormy was big and strong by looking at him. But he didn't find out until later exactly how strong the boy was. Imagine the captain's surprise when he discovered Stormy was so strong he could lift himself to the crow's nest by pulling up on his coat collar!

4.

The Foggy Stew

The *Lady of the Sea* was in the China trade. She was fully loaded with timber, metal goods, cotton cloth and notions. When she cast off the wind filled her sails, and soon the land was left far behind.

On the outward voyage the ship became becalmed in the doldrums. For days she lay silent in a fog, with never a cat's paw of wind.

The fog grew thicker. "It's the worst fog I ever saw," declared Captain Hardstone.

There seemed to be no sun or moon or stars. There seemed to be no day or night. Nothing but a gray curtain of fog. There seemed to be no fore or aft, no up or down.

"The only way you can tell up from down," said the captain, "is to drop something. When it hits your foot, you can tell that way is down."

The fog got thicker still. "This ain't no pea soup fog," said the captain. "It's thicker than that."

24

"Speaking of pea soup, that's an uncommon good smell coming from the galley," said Stormalong.

"So it is. But it ain't pea soup. It's plum duff," said the captain. "A heaven touched mixture of flour, water, and prunes."

"What's that?" asked Stormalong.

"Plum duff," said the captain.

"No. I know what plum duff is. I mean, what's that noise?"

Captain Hardstone cocked his head to listen better. "It's a kind of a flutterin' sound," he said.

"It's fish. That's what it is. It's fish! There are fish swimming in the fog!" said Stormalong.

"Fish?" the captain was puzzled.

Stormalong listened again. Then slowly the facts came to his mind, and as they did, he put them into words. "This fog is so thick a man can't tell where the water stops and the fog begins. So it stands to reason that a fish, which is no ways as smart as a man, can't tell either."

"Yes sir, it stands to reason. It certainly does," the captain muttered, still wondering how this strange fact could be true, as it undoubtedly was, and at the same time admiring Stormy for his quick logic and clear explanation.

Stormy continued. "They smell the plum duff cooking. It smells so good, they are swimming for it."

25

When he heard his own words, Stormy got an idea. Peering through the fog, he was dimly able to see a school of salmon nosing around the cracks at the edge of the galley door.

Softly he glided to the starboard porthole of the galley. "Cookie, are you there?" he whispered.

"Yes," the cook answered. "I shut the galley door so as to try to keep some of the fog out."

"You're keeping the salmon out too," Stormy told him.

"What?" The wonder in the cook's voice made it clear that he was not following Stormy.

"There are salmon sniffing at the galley door. They smell your plum duff cooking."

"Most everybody likes my plum duff," the cook said with pride in his voice. There was a pause. "But—fish! I never heard of fish caring one way or another about plum duff. As a matter of fact, I never heard of fish sniffing around a galley door!"

"Just take my word for it," said Stormy. "Listen. Put some plum duff in a big cooking pot, the biggest one you've got."

"Well, I don't know what you've got in mind. But I'll do what you say," the cook answered.

When the pot was ready, Stormalong opened the galley door. The salmon swam inside. They swam directly toward the plum duff in the pot.

26

Stormy followed closely behind them. Fortunately the salmon were so intent on the delicious smelling plum duff, they ignored all signs of danger and forgot caution. They swam right into the waiting pot and greedily began to munch at the tasty plum duff.

Stormy stepped forward and slammed the lid on the pot. "Got 'em!" he declared.

The salmon were poached in the pot full of fog, and all the sailors agreed they had never had better poached salmon. And the plum duff was the perfect dessert for such a delicious meal.

Stormalong met the captain after dinner on the quarter deck. There was a happy, contented look in Captain Hardstone's eyes. "I do declare, that was the best poached salmon I ever put a tooth to. I tell you it makes a big difference when fish are fresh caught."

But the contentment did not last. A man can't remember a pleasant meal forever. Work must be done, and the captain was restless at the long delay in the fog. He tried to peer through the gray curtain that enveloped the ship, examining every quarter for a sign of a breeze.

But the sails hung limp, with no flap or flutter. She was a silent ship on a silent sea—as quiet as an eel swimming in oil.

"I certainly would admire to see a sign of a breeze," Captain Hardstone said. "I'd welcome any wind able to move, even enough to ripple up a fly's eyelashes would give me hope."

"Maybe I can help," said Stormalong.

"Poached salmon is fine, and I like it. I would enjoy eating a good many meals of it. But it's wind I want, boy." Captain Hardstone moved to the rail and stared over it into the gray fog. The captain was now a solemn man.

"That's what I mean," said Stormy. He turned and walked to the stern of the ship. Facing the bow, he planted his feet firmly on the planks that were wet from the dripping fog. He squared his shoulders, took a deep breath, and blew.

The slack sails fluttered a small flutter. "There's a show of a breeze," Captain Hardstone cried.

Stormy took another deep breath. His chest expanded and three buttons popped off and danced across the wet planks.

"What are you doing there, boy?" the captain shouted.

Stormy didn't answer. He blew again. The sails bent out.

"Never seen anything like it before," the captain exclaimed. "Man and boy, I never seen—"

His words were lost in the breeze as Stormy blew again. A small white crest began to trail along each side of the prow, as the *Lady of the Sea* moved slowly through the water.

The ship picked up speed. The prow pushed the seas aside.

Captain Hardstone and the crew watched with amazement as Stormy blew the fog away. He blew the ship right out of the doldrums and into the trade winds.

When the breeze of nature caught the sails, Stormy stopped his blowing. To tell the truth, his face was red, and he sat down because he needed a rest. But he soon caught his breath and grinned, well satisfied with what he had done.

"Hip, hip!" the captain cried.

"Hooray!" the crew replied.

"Stormalong!"

"Stormalong!"

Captain Hardstone promoted Stormy and made him boatswain. When he blew his boatswain's whistle he blew it so loud the echo would dry the sailors' laundry on a rainy day.

5.

The Sleigh Ride

After several voyages aboard the *Lady of the Sea,* Stormy decided he had to find a bigger ship. He was still a boy, just verging on manhood, but he was more than several times as big as most men, so he needed a ship more than several times as big as most ships.

He couldn't find one that was that big, but he signed up as boatswain with a whaler, the *Greasy Ann,* Captain Stern-buck, master.

When the lookout in the crow's nest high above the deck saw a whale, he would shout, "Thar she blows!" Every sailor would strain his eyes to see the whale.

"Where away?" the master would reply.

"Off the port bow, nor' by nor'east!"

Then came the order, "Lower the boats!" The men would spring to their posts. The boats would be lowered, the men would pull on the oars, and the whaleboats would toss in the swelling sea as they made their way toward the whale, the earth's largest creature.

When a boat reached a whale, the harpooner threw his pointed and barbed weapon. With good aim and force, it would cut through the tough skin and sink deep into the creature's flesh.

A long rope, fastened to the harpoon, would uncoil as the injured whale tried to escape. When enough rope was played out, it was tied to the boat, and the boat would be pulled through the water at a dizzy speed by the angry whale, in what the sailors called a Nantucket sleigh ride. The whale-boat was often pulled a great many miles from the ship.

After months, even years, at sea, when the holds were full of oil, whalebone, and ambergris, the ship would set out for its distant home port. Then she was called a greasy ship, and a greasy ship was a good ship, for with it went money for the owners and the crew.

There was danger and hard work and excitement in a whaler man's life, more than several times as much as most men wanted, and therefore almost enough for Stormalong.

The *Greasy Ann* had a good, greasy voyage, thanks to the prowess of Stormalong. She was loaded to the gunwales. There wasn't room for another drop of oil or another pound of bone or ambergris.

Then a storm struck. She was a Cape Horn snorter. Captain Sternbuck stood on his quarter deck, a worried man. "In twenty years at sea, I never saw such a storm. She's a blowin' so hard she could blow the hair off a dog," he said.

Stormalong had seen quite a lot of wind in his day too, and he quite agreed with the captain.

"Call all hands and the cook!" the captain ordered. "Man the pumps! Reef the sails!"

The wind blew so hard it blew the buttons off the sailors' shirts, but they bravely went about their work with their shirt tails flapping in the wind.

No men ever worked harder. The heavy ship tossed like a cork. The main top gallant split. The foretop mizzen sail yielded to the gale with a bang. The flying jib followed, and the torn canvas sailed away as fast as a witch on a broom stick.

One by one the other sails blew out. The ship was down to her bare poles. She tossed stem to stern. She tossed port to starboard.

"She's takin' water at a scandalous rate," the mate cried.

The wind blew the knot holes out of the starboard side of the galley.

It was a desperate time but, as all things must come to an end, the storm passed. "How's the ship?" the exhausted captain inquired.

"She's all in one piece—what there is left of her," said Storm-along.

"One piece," Captain Sternbuck echoed forlornly. "One piece. But she's without a stitch of canvas to catch the wind, and she is doomed, as we are all doomed, to languish and die on this lonely sea. Doomed! D'you hear? Doomed!" the captain was growing hysterical. The hurricane-harried veteran of a thousand gales was nearly a broken man.

Stormy felt sorry for the poor fellow. He tried to put a note of brightness into his voice. "A school of right whales is coming up off the stern on the port side," he said.

"Bosun Stormalong," the captain cried, "our holds are full of oil. We are a greasy ship. We need no more blubber!"

Stormalong saw it was useless to discuss the matter further. The whales were coming even with the ship and soon would pass her. Stormy ran forward and, standing on the prow, called out, "Avast. Hand me a harpoon!"

The mate, moving automatically, obeyed the command of a man who was born to command. He brought a harpoon and thrust it into Stormalong's waiting hand. It was a harpoon that had been especially made for Stormy. It was more than several times larger than most harpoons.

Stormy lifted the big harpoon and cast it at one of the largest whales in the passing school.

Whirrrrr. The rope uncoiled as the harpoon sped through the air.

Zip! Thud! The barbed point sank into the giant creature. It lashed its flukes in the water and surged forward.

"Another!" cried Stormy.

Another harpoon was placed in his hand. Whirrrrr. Zip! Thud!

"Another!"

Whirrrrr. Zip! Thud!

Harpoons, one after another, sank into ten whales. Giant flukes churned the water as the whales plowed ahead.

"Take a hitch of those lines around the capstan," Stormy directed.

Eight lines were tightened around the heavy iron post. Stormy held two of the rope lines in his hands. Half a score of right whales, the largest creatures on the globe, pulled, and the *Greasy Ann* acted like she had a bone in her teeth. White foam formed as the prow split the deep, blue water.

Captain Sternbuck came on the run. "What are you doing?" he cried.

"I'm fixing for the biggest Nantucket sleigh ride any one ever had!" Stormalong answered and the ship started to move as fast as a cat when a dog barks.

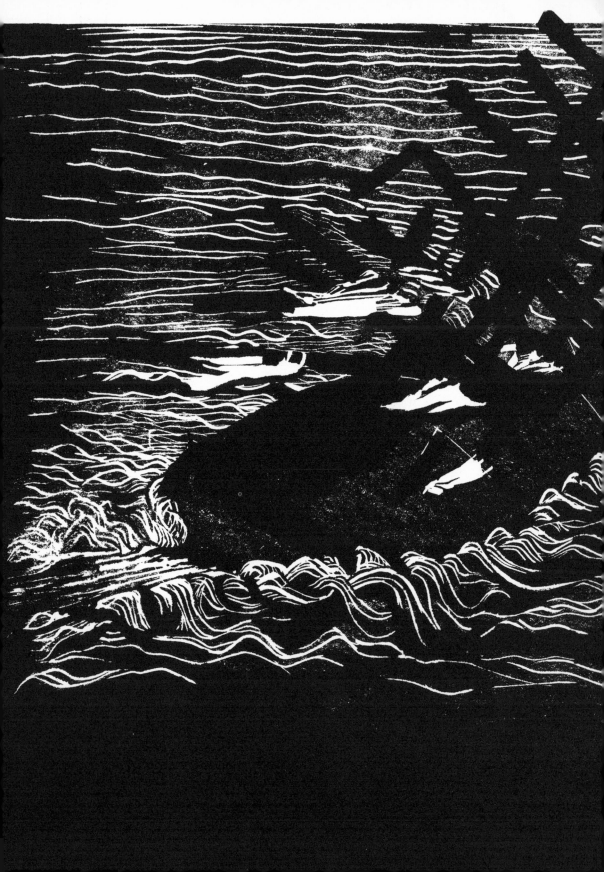

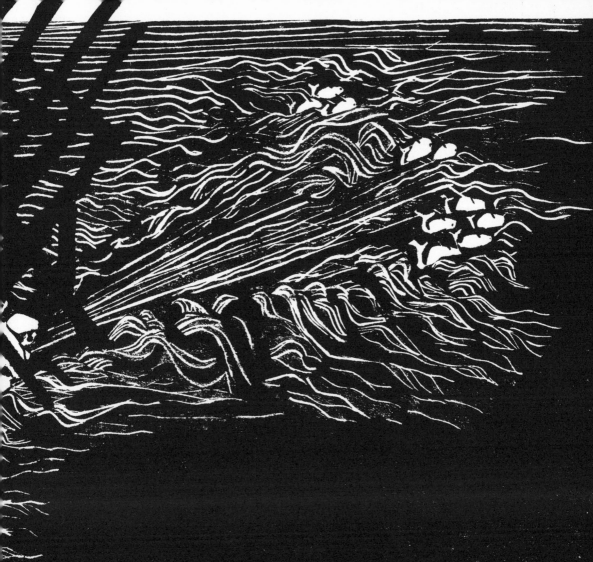

"A Nantucket sleigh ride!" a sailor shouted.

"Wheeee!" another cried.

All of the sailors had been thrown head over heels by the sudden start, but they scrambled to their feet and ran to the rails where they could hang on and watch the fun as the whales churned through the water.

Stormalong guided the whales as they drew the boat at a speed that broke all records.

37

"What's that back there?" the captain suddenly asked.

"What? Where?" Stormy inquired.

"Back there. Straight off the stern," said the captain as he pointed toward a dark shadow that seemed to be following the *Greasy Ann*.

Stormy was puzzled. "It looks like a shadow and it has the shape of a ship. You can see a trace of reddish brown at the water line," he said.

"So it does, so it is and so you can," the captain agreed. "But what is it?"

"It looks like nothing I ever saw before," said Stormy. "But it has the shape of a ship, and she shows that reddish color at the water line, just like the *Greasy Ann*." Stormy paused a moment. Suddenly he said, "I know. I know what it is!"

"What?" the captain asked.

"It's paint."

"Paint?"

"Yes. It's paint," Stormy declared. "These whales started off so fast, they pulled the Greasy Ann right out of her coat of paint!"

The captain leaned over the rail and swept his eyes along the side of the ship. When he turned back to the boatswain his face was ashen. "You're right," he said. "The paint is gone. She's stripped down to the bare wood!"

The ten whales kept their speed up in the days and nights that followed and Stormalong never left his post. No one else was able to guide the giant creatures as they plowed through the water, pulling the *Greasy Ann* behind them.

When he made a landfall, Stormy guided the whales along

38

the coast and into the harbor.

"You done it, Mister Stormalong!" Captain Sternbuck shouted. "You brought her in, bung up and bilge free and loaded with oil!"

Some sailors still say there is a phantom ship roaming in the Atlantic. They say they often see her dimly. She seems to be a dark shape with a red-brown color at the water line— just like the coat of paint that was stripped off the *Greasy Ann* when Stormalong took her on a ten whale Nantucket sleigh ride.

6.
Stormy Swallows The Anchor

Stormalong became discouraged with his life at sea. He loved the ocean, he loved ships and the sailor's life, for he had salt water in his blood. But he decided to stop sailing. He would swallow the anchor, as sailors said when they decided to take up a landlubber's life. It was a heartbreaking decision.

Some people wondered how Stormalong could give up the sea. The plain truth is that it was because of his size. Ships were not big enough for him. He was so big he couldn't get into a sailor's hammock, and he felt he couldn't go through life sleeping on an open deck with his feet poking over the side. It annoyed him when the gulls came to roost on them.

Indeed, it was his size that gave rise to some of the fashions in sailors' clothing. He was so tall he had to stand on a stool to button his shirt collar. He felt conspicuous doing this, and besides, there wasn't always a stool handy. He began wearing a shirt with a V collar and no button.

Then too, he was so tall he had to get down on his knees to put his hands in his pockets. This was inconvenient, so he had his pants made without pockets.

Because other sailors wanted to be as much like Stormy as they could, they copied these styles, and that is the reason why today sailors' pants have no pockets and why they wear V neck shirts.

Stormy told his friends, "Yes. I'm going to swallow the anchor."

"Where are you going?" one asked.

"I don't know for sure. But I know what I'm going to do," he said.

"What?"

"I'm going to a place where no one knows anything about life at sea."

"How are you going to do that?"

Stormalong picked up an oar. "I'm going to put this oar on my shoulder. Then I'm going to start walking west. When I get so far away from the ocean that no one knows what an oar is, that's where I'll stop. That's where I'll work and build me a new life."

"You'll be back, Stormy," his friends said. "You'll be back. You couldn't leave the sea any more than you could quit breathin'."

"Nope. I'm swallowing the anchor. Now." He shouldered his oar, and his long, rolling strides soon took him over the hills and out of sight.

Every now and then when he met someone on the road, he would pause, point to his oar and ask, "Do you know what this is?"

When the answer was, "An oar," he would move on, muttering, "Not far enough. Not far enough from the ocean yet. I've got to go further or someone will always remind me of my life at sea. If I can't be a sailor and sleep in a bed or a hammock like other people do, I want to forget all about it."

When he was far enough away from the ocean, he didn't need to ask. A farmer standing by the side of the road asked him: "Pardon me stranger, is that thing you are carrying over your shoulder some new kind of a flail or something?"

"No sir. It's an oar," said Stormalong.

"What's an oar for?" the farmer asked.

"Well, I might use it for a flail some time," said Stormy, and he proceeded to swallow the anchor. He knew he was now far enough away from the ocean.

He started his new job as a farmer with grim determination.

Now his world was not as large as the ocean, where the ever receding horizon constantly met his gaze. Now his world was closed by surrounding hills and trees. But he thought he might become accustomed to it. He wasn't quite so sure about becoming accustomed to the problems of farming, however.

First, there was the rain. It didn't make water a man could sail on. It made mud. Deep, heavy, soggy mud. He was a heavy man, and one day, after a week of steady rain, he sank in the mud. It acted almost like quick sand. Deeper and deeper he sank, until he was up to his arm pits in the ooze, and he was stuck fast.

He was all alone, and it was growing dark. It seemed to be hopeless, and he cried for help. He had never doubted that some day he might have a watery grave, but mud . . . ugh.

If only he had a shovel. No one came to help him. Suddenly he was ashamed. He had cried for help. He had never done such a thing at sea. He resolved he would never do it again.

He was thoroughly ashamed. He was so ashamed that he went home and got a shovel and came back and shoveled himself out of the mud.

When winter came he was not prepared because he hadn't become a farmer until late summer. He had no crops to harvest, other than some late turnips, and they did little towards filling his ample stomach.

Stormalong was a good marksman, but there was not much game. To make matters worse he was running low on bullets.

When he was down to his last bullet he saw a flock of pigeons fly into the yard and settle on the limb of a tree. He counted them. There were thirty-seven pigeons, and he needed them. Every one of them. He know if he shot his gun he could get one pigeon, but the noise would frighten away the others.

It took him only a moment to decide what to do. He would not use his last bullet. Carefully, he poured a load of powder down the gun barrel. After he had packed the powder, he stuffed his open jack knife down the barrel and moved into good shooting position.

Carefully he brought the long rifle to his shoulder. His eye lined the sights. He squeezed the trigger.

Bang!

The noise shattered the silence of the quiet grove.

Thirty-seven pairs of wings fluttered wildly, but not one
bird left the tree limb. His aim had been true. The blade of
his jack knife had split the limb and thirty-seven pigeons'
toes were firmly caught in the crack!

Thirty-seven pigeons didn't keep a big man going for long,
but with them he was able to piece out a few small meals.

He spent his last bullet on larger game, and when that was
gone he turned to rabbits.

Stormy's method of catching rabbits was a simple one. He
painted a rock black, and then threw it into the snow. When
he saw a rabbit going in that direction, he waited until the
creature was near the rock. Then he shouted and ran toward
the rabbit.

The cotton tail, thinking the rock was a hole, would dive for it, and knock itself out.

Stormalong lived the rest of the winter on rabbits.

The fall and winter had been bad, but the following summer was worse.

There was no rain, and there were no crops. The pigs got so thin it took two of them to throw a shadow. Stormy had to tie knots in their tails to keep them from crawling through the cracks in the fence.

The pigs became so weak they fell over when they tried to pull up a blade of grass. They were so fragile that when they grunted they had to lean up against a tree and rest for a while.

The creek was so dry the fish had to stand on their heads to keep their gills wet. The potatoes were smaller than the little end of nothing.

It would have been a dull summer except for a lizard in the backyard. It was interesting to see how he survived. Everyone knows a lizard can grow a new tail, and the lizard in the backyard lived on his tail. When he was hungry he ate it. And then, in the course of a few days he grew a new tail, which provided him with another dinner the next time he got hungry.

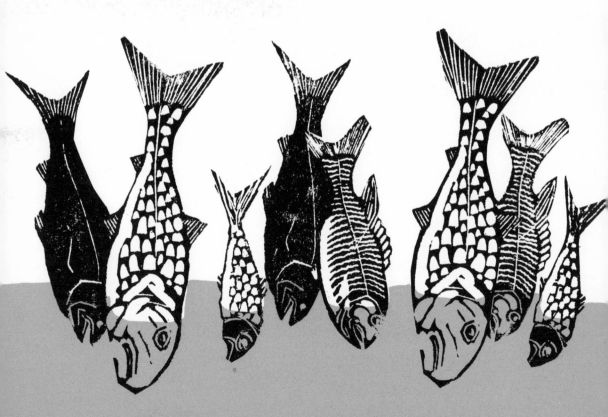

7.

The Dark Cliffs Of Dover

Stormalong soon realized that a farmer's life was not the life for him. He longed for the rolling sea, the feel of a moving ship beneath his feet and of salt spray in his face.

As he had once decided to quit the sea, he now decided to leave the land. A ship that was too small, an awkward ship, any vessel, any life on the ocean, anything about a sailor's life was better than everything about a farmer's life.

The news of his return to tidewater went before him. "Mister Stormalong is coming," they said.

"Old Stormalong is coming."

"Stormy is coming back to the sea."

One person passed the news on to another, and when he stood on the last rise of land and saw the ocean before him, a great smile of satisfaction spread over his face. He should never have gone away from the sea. He should never have swallowed the anchor. Now he knew the truth. He was born for the sea. Didn't he have salt water in his blood?

He was greeted with cheers and shouts of welcome and a surprise. The ship owners had banded together to build a

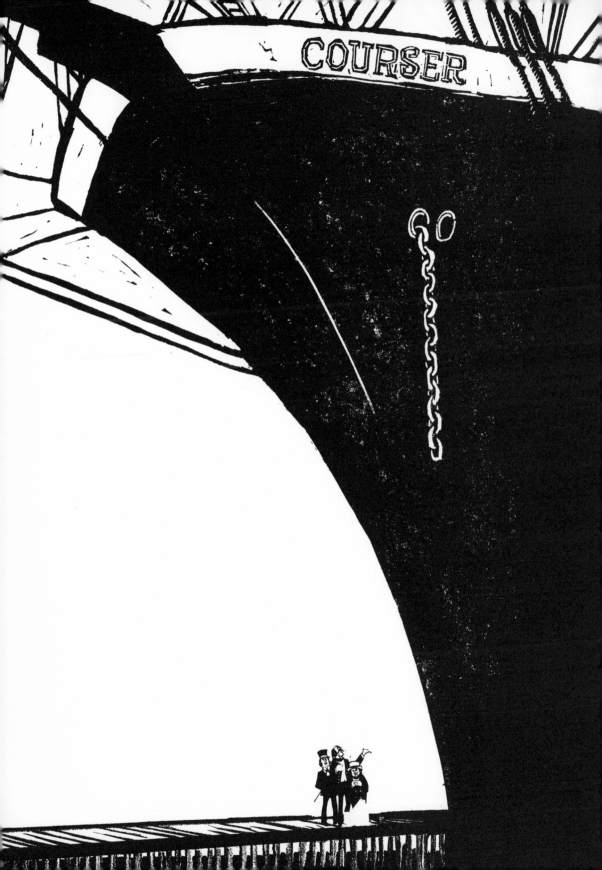

ship that was big enough for Stormalong. She was in the harbor waiting for him. Her name was *Courser*, and because Stormalong was more than several times bigger than most men, the *Courser* was more than several times bigger than most ships.

Stormalong was to be her captain. Captain Alfred Bulltop Stormalong!

The crew was more than several times larger than most crews. The wheel was more than several times bigger than most wheels. Fortunately she kept a steady course, and in light seas and gentle breezes several men could handle the helm. But in heavy seas and strong winds only Captain Stormalong could manage the wheel.

Fast horses were on board to carry the crew from stem to stern when the watches were changed. The *Courser* was so big she couldn't get into most harbors. In some harbors she had to back in or back out, because they weren't big enough for her to turn around in.

The masts were so tall they were hinged in the middle so they could be folded back to let the moon go by. The tips of the masts and spars were round at the ends so they wouldn't punch holes in the rain clouds.

One time, in the North Sea, when Captain Stormalong was asleep in the cabin, the weather got dirty. There were more than several men at the wheel, but they were not strong enough to control the ship, and she headed for the English Channel. It was a sudden change in weather, and by the time Stormalong woke up and got on deck it was too late.

"Avast, you lubbers, where are you taking her?" he cried.

"She's in the English Channel, sir," one of the men said.

"She's too broad of beam to go through the channel!" old Stormalong roared, with a roar loud enough to rise above the growing storm and even make it falter for a moment. He seized the wheel, but it was too late to turn, and she couldn't escape the gale that was pelting her.

"Shall I tell the crew to man the life boats?" the mate asked nervously.

"Never!" cried Stormalong.

"But we can't make the channel," the mate said.

"Never say 'can't,'" Stormalong answered as he peered through the heavy weather. His eyes roamed over the surface of the angry sea.

"The tide is high," he muttered.

"The wind is high too. I suggest we take to the life boats," said the mate.

Stormalong seemed not to hear the mate's voice. "With such a high tide, we might sneak through. We just might," he said half to himself.

His moment of quiet thought passed. He had made up his mind. Now he was a man of action. "Call all hands and the cook," he roared.

His eyes narrowed as he studied the desperate situation. "I've got to go through. It's our only chance." He clamped his teeth together, and the masseter muscles on his jaws swelled out as big as apple halves.

"All hands and the cook on deck!" the mate bellowed.

The sailors fell to and stood at their posts, waiting breathlessly, as the ship approached the narrow part of the channel. Calais was on the French coast, and the Dark Cliffs of Dover rose from the water on the English side.

"It's going to be a close shave," said Stormalong, as the ship bent to the wind and the rigging sang like a thousand fiddles' crescendo.

The Dark Cliffs of Dover grew close. Old Stormalong moved the wheel an inch this way, half an inch that way. The currents swirled, and the waves beat against the ship's hull.

"We ain't a goin' to make it," the mate said, and his hands trembled.

"There is only one chance," said Stormalong. "Pay out all the soap in the storerooms and pay out the load of soap we have in the forward hold."

"Soap?" Wonder replaced fear in the mate's soul.

"Yes, soap, Mister Mate! The soap in the stores and the soap in the forward hold that we took aboard in Denmark!"

53

There was no mistaking the command, and the mate, still puzzled, relayed the order to the waiting crew.

When the soap was on deck, the sailors stood speechless with wonder, and fear filled their bones. It was a bad position, and if their captain had gone mad, they were lost—and who but a mad man could order all that soap on deck at such a time?

Stormalong looked down on the waiting men and the soap. "Every three men rig a bosun's chair!" he ordered.

The sailors all sprang to the task, and in short order the deck was filled with boatswain's chairs. Short boards were rigged in a knotted rope hoop in such a fashion as to form a seat. Such seats, hanging at the end of a rope, were used as places for sailors to sit while working on a mast or on the side of the ship.

"Now, over the sides," roared old Stormalong, and his voice drowned out the wind. "Over the side with those bosun's chairs and buckets of soap, and swab her sides with soap. Put it on good and thick!"

Driven by the force of their captain's commands, the sailors followed orders and painted the sides of the ship with soap.

They finished just in time. The Dark Cliffs of Dover were approaching. As the men pulled the bosun's chairs back onto the deck, the ship rubbed against the cliff's face. But the crash of timber they were all expecting never came. Instead, there was a gentle shwishshshshshsh.

54

The soaped ship was sliding smoothly through the narrow part of the channel between the Dark Cliffs of Dover and the coast of France!

It took one hour for the great ship to slip past the Dark Cliffs of Dover with Old Stormalong at the helm, turning the wheel a bit this way, half a bit the other way, and a quarter of a bit back.

When the hour of bone-chilling danger was past, the sailors looked back. "Look!" cried the mate. "The Dark Cliffs of Dover are white!"

"It's the soap," said Captain Stormalong. "It rubbed off on the Dark Cliffs and changed their color. Washed them clean and bleached them white. From now on the Dark Cliffs of Dover will be the White Cliffs of Dover."

The White Cliffs of Dover remain to this day as a monument to Captain Alfred Bulltop Stormalong. It was only because of the high tide, the soap, and Stormalong's skill that the ship was saved. Any one who cares to look may still see the foam from the soap in the swirling waters at the base of the White Cliffs.

8.
A Grand Old Skipper

In the days when Stormalong sailed the *Courser*, the seas were not charted as they are now, and it was necessary for a captain to use great ingenuity to protect his ship. The sailors said that Stormalong knew the sea so well he could recognize each wave, and that he could sail by the seat of his pants.

The depth of the water was tested by dropping a lead weight which was attached to a rope. When the lead reached bottom, it was pulled up, and the depth was measured by knots or marks on the rope. The sailors said that Stormalong could tell where he was by the taste of the small grains of ocean bottom which clung to the lead.

57

They tell a story about one time when the *Courser* was in the North Atlantic, and a hurricane struck. It was a real snorter. The wind changed directions so fast the needle dropped off the compass. The clouds were so heavy a man couldn't see his hand in front of his face in the daytime and at night it was as dark as the inside of a whale.

In such a blow Stormalong ordered the plumb line dropped over the side to test the depth and to find out where the ship was. There was no other way to tell her location.

The sailor pulled in the plumb line. "She's in sixteen fathoms of water, sir," he said.

Stormalong took the lead. He rubbed some of the grit that had stuck to it between his fingers as he smelled the lead and put his tongue to it. "We are twenty-seven leagues south-south-west of Cape Cod," he said.

That evening when the sailor pulled in the sounding line, he said, "Eight fathoms of water, sir."

Stormalong sniffed the lead and tasted it. "We are two leagues south-southwest of Cape Cod," he said solemnly.

The hurricane continued to lash at the ship. The *Courser* was turned and tossed by constantly changing wind and tides.

58

Again the Stormalong spoke to the sailor, "Take another sounding," he ordered.

The sailor dropped the sounding line over the side and pulled it in. "Only three fathoms of water, sir," he said through frightened lips.

Stormalong sniffed and tasted the lead. "If it were not for the blackness of the night we would be in clear sight of Cape Cod," he said.

Stormalong was worried. He knew he could sail in less water than other captains, for he remembered the time he sailed half a mile in a heavy dew, but the situation was dangerous. In such a storm there was nothing to be done but sail the ship as well as he could. "Take another sounding," he commanded.

The sailor followed orders and dropped the line over the rail. Hurriedly he drew it back and turned to the captain. "We are in half a fathom of water, sir," he mumbled fearfully.

It was bad news. Stormalong frowned as he took the lead from the man's trembling hands. He sniffed and tasted. His frown deepened. He sniffed and tasted again.

"It can't be!" he muttered. "It can't be!"

"What can't be, sir?" the frightened sailor asked.

Stormalong rolled some of the grit between his fingers. Every sense was alert. Carefully he smelled the lead again, and he put his tongue to it with greatest deliberation. "Thunder and tarnation!" he bellowed in his foghorn voice, and its sound seemed to silence the howling wind for a moment.

"What—what is it, sir?" the sailor asked anxiously.

Stormalong was about to shout again, but he remembered his foghorn voice and spoke calmly. "I don't understand this at all, not at all," he said, "for by the smell and taste of the lead we are over Cape Cod, and we are passing directly over the Widow Johnstone's cabbage patch, three miles east of Yarmouth, and south-southwest of Barnstable harbor!"

When day broke the weather was clear, and Stormalong took his bearings with the sunrise. The *Courser* was in Cape Cod Bay, just outside of Barnstable harbor.

"It was a wild night we passed though, and how we got into Cape Cod Bay I do not know for sure," Stormalong said thoughtfully. "But we certainly didn't go around the point of Cape Cod, and I am sure we must have passed directly over Cape Cod and over the Widow Johnstone's cabbage patch, for I never make a mistake in the taste and smell of the lead."

Later in the day Stormalong disembarked and while walking down the street in Yarmouth he met the Widow Johnstone. "Oh, Captain Stormalong," she said. "The strangest thing happened last night. The tides were the highest I have ever seen, and of course it can't be true, because such a thing never happened before, but in the middle of the night I could have sworn that a big ship passed by my house and went right over my cabbage patch, and that I heard your voice shout 'thunder and tarnation.' It was such a dark night I couldn't see anything, but I feel sure it was your voice. 'Thunder and tarnation' were the words I heard, and I heard them just as clear as could be. Do you suppose I could have been dreaming?"

Stormalong didn't want to deceive her, nor did he want to tell her the truth because the poor soul would fret and worry if she knew ships could pass so near her house. Moreover she would tell others, and Stormalong would be the center of attention. He was a modest man and tried to avoid being recognized as a hero whenever he could. So he patted the Widow Johnstone's hand gently. "Strange things sometimes happen in a hurricane, Mrs. Johnstone," he said.

The story probably never would have been known if the sailor who handled the lead hadn't told some of his shipmates. Of course they told others, and now this remarkable incident has been added to the store of remarkable incidents known about the life of that greatest of all sea captains, Alfred Bulltop Stormalong.

Stormalong sailed the *Courser* for many years, carrying freight and passengers all over the world, and long before the end of his lifetime he was recognized by all as the greatest sailor ever to sail the Seven Seas.

Sailors have created a chanty about him which they sing while at work. It raises their spirits. It makes them realize that tasks which seem impossible are made possible when men work hard and when they work together.

The words of the chanty recall to them the great days of sailing ships, the days of wooden ships and iron men, and of the greatest sailor of them all, Stormalong. As they work to-gether they sing the chanty, and its rhythm is the pulse that marks the time as they push at the capstan and pump handles, as they pull on ropes and do the hard work that keeps the ship afloat and cargoes moving.

Old Stormalong was a grand old man,
  To my way, hey, Stormalong.
Old Stormalong was a grand old man,
  To my way, hey, Stormalong.

An able seaman, bold and true,
  To my way, hey, Stormalong.
A good old skipper to his crew,
  To my way, hey, Stormalong.

Old Stormy was a sailor bold,
  To my way, hey, Stormalong.
A grand old man in days of old,
  To my way, hey, Stormalong.

For many years he sailed the seas,
  To my way, hey, Stormalong.
In heavy storm and gentle breeze,
  To my way, hey, Stormalong.

Now Stormy's gone, a good old man,
  To my way, hey, Stormalong.
We'll never see his like again,
  To my way, hey, Stormalong.